LITTLE SIMON

An imprint of Simon & Schuster Children's Publishing Division

1230 Avenue of the Americas, New York, New York 10020

Text copyright © 2013 by Alison Reynolds. Illustrations copyright © 2013 by Heath McKenzie.
First published by The Five Mile Press 2013. First Little Simon hardcover edition 2014.

All rights reserved, including the right of reproduction in whole or in part in any form.
LITTLE SIMON is a registered trademark of Simon & Schuster, Inc., and associated
colophon is a trademark of Simon & Schuster, Inc.

For information about special discounts for bulk purchases, please contact Simon & Schuster
Special Sales at 1-866-506-1949 or business@simonandschuster.com.

The Simon & Schuster Speakers Bureau can bring authors to your live event.

For more information or to book an event contact the Simon & Schuster Speakers Bureau at
1-866-248-3049 or visit our website at www.simonspeakers.com.

Manufactured in China 0514 FMP

10 9 8 7 6 5 4 3 2 1

Library of Congress Cataloging-in-Publication Data

Reynolds, Alison, 1962–

A new friend for Marmalade / by Alison Reynolds ; illustrated by Heath McKenzie.

— 1st Little Simon ed.

pages cm

"First published by The Five Mile Press 2013."

Summary: Maddy, Ella and Marmalade are friends, but when the boy across the road tries
to join in their fun, the girls are reluctant to let him play. A story about accepting new friends.

ISBN 978-1-4814-2046-4 (hardcover picture book) [1. Friendship—Fiction. 2. Cats—Fiction.]

I. McKenzie, Heath, illustrator.

II. Title.

PZPZ7.R3334New 2013

[E]—dc23

2013044215

NOV 0 3 2014

a new
friend
for
marmalade

ALISON REYNOLDS • HEATH McKENZIE

LITTLE SIMON

New York   London   Toronto   Sydney   New Delhi

Ella, Maddy, and Marmalade were
best friends.

One morning, as the sun warmed their backs, they decided to build a playhouse.

Toby, the boy from across the road, joined in.

Ella SHRUGGED and Maddy sighed....

Marmalade peeped out in surprise.

So the girls decided to build
a **sand-castle city** instead, with wondrous
TOWERs
and tunnels, with roads and **RIVERS**.

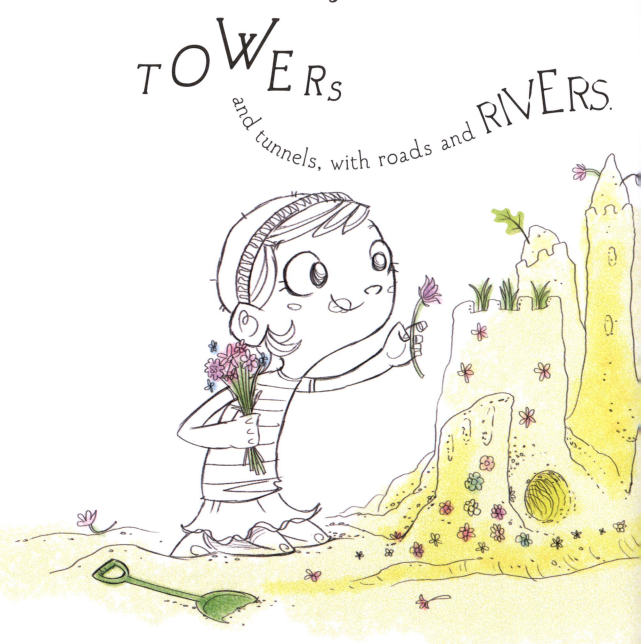

Marmalade lolled in the sun, watching
the girls smooth down the sand, until...

... a **whirlwind** cartwheeled through the sandpit. Maddy scowled and Ella frowned.

Marmalade *rubbed* his head against Toby.

Toby knelt and patted the cat.
"You're **STROKING** his fur the **wrong** way," muttered Ella.

Marmalade rolled over and Purred.

That afternoon,

Maddy and Ella rebuilt their ruined city.
They repaired every bridge.
They reshaped every tower.
They even added a **moat.**

"I'll fill the moat," said Toby.

Toby jumped up and **TWISTED** on the faucet.

Marmalade **leaped** into the tree as the lawn erupted into FOUNTAINS of water.

Maddy **HUMpHED** and Ella **GRUmPED.** **SHIVERING,** the girls dried themselves in the sunshine.

High up in the tree...

Marmalade slunk farther and
farther along a branch,
chasing the last rays of sun, when...

CRACK!

The branch TREMBLED in the breeze. Marmalade let out a small scared meow.

Maddy STRETCHED up.
"I'll catch you."
Marmalade's claws tightly gripped the branch.

"Leap onto the rake!" shouted Ella. Marmalade swung slowly back and forth. He clung on **tighter** and **tighter**.

Toby whipped off his cape.
"Grab a corner," he said to the girls.
Then he shouted to Marmalade, "JUMP!"

Marmalade
squeezed
his
eyes
shut
and
let
go.

Next morning, there was no playhouse, there were no bridges or towers or moats.

Ella, Maddy, and Toby played
a new game, and they all wore capes...

even Marmalade.